Music for the Dream

Music for the Dream

Seven Short Stories

by Valerie Haynes Perry

ISBN: 978-0-578-02267-3

Cover design and interior text design by The Word Process

Cover photograph by Frederick Douglass Perry

Fiction/Literature/African-American Fiction

Third Edition, 2009

Music for the Dream is available at lulu.com

Also by the author:

Tanner Blue

Table of Contents

Dedication

For those who listen deeply, hearing only truth

El niño

El niño prowled around the Berkeley Hills, seeking shelter from his storm. Nerves rattled, the forming infant pressed a heavy hand on one pitched roof and stopped a while to rest. Without regret, this wayward child of wind and rain stole one small corner of the night from the man, Nash, and the woman, Joana, lying inside that house—side by side, his browner skin inches from hers, touchable—on a bed of cooling sweat.

Nash Ambrose dreamed heavily in fields of midnight dew that skipped back to his tenth year. He walked his shiny, red, three-speed bike beside his father in East River Park on the Lower East Side of Manhattan across F.D.R. Drive, which lined the projects where they lived. Nash's heart thumped because the very first weekend he did not ask his father to take him to the park was the one that delivered his wish. Up until then, his father had always been too tired, too angry, or too tired of being angry to say, "Yes."

It was mid autumn, the musty incense of burning leaves pungent in the steel-cool morning air. The sun crowned, burnt orange, above the Domino Sugar sign that marked the distant, Brooklyn side of the Williamsburg Bridge. Passing through the latticed shadow cast by its span, Justus Ambrose took a nip from a bottle of Gordon's gin wrapped neatly in its transparent brown paper bag. He followed it with a growling, "Aaaaaagh," and wiped his mouth with the denim cuffs of both sleeves.

Unable to stomach his father's after-breakfast snack, Nash skipped his left foot on one pedal of the bike, slung his right leg over the seat, and took off south. Timing himself, he rode to the end of the park marked by a fire station, speeding past the community clinic where survivors, witnesses, and bystanders told ghost stories about teeth pulled without Novocain, wounds dressed lacking antiseptics, and whimsical surgeries. Slowing his pace, Nash rode as far as the Fulton Street fish market, glimpsing a partial view of the tawny Brooklyn Bridge before turning back.

As soon as he was again within the boundaries of the park, Nash saw his father sitting on a bench with its peeling green paint, arms spread like bent wings over its back. One long, thin, muscular leg was crossed over the other, swinging, swinging, back and forth. He waved at Nash and had another nip and growl.

Nash joined his father, crossing his own chubby legs, hurling one fleshy arm along their bench's back. They sat there, both looking in the general direction of the tight-lipped Statue of Liberty, praying for a new kind of weather. Slowly, Nash turned and looked up at his dad, whose bronze face seemed too thin. The spots of gray at his temples and in his trimmed mustache caught Nash off guard—he had always thought of his father as older, never old. All too often, the crevices of his elder's eyes caved in to southern nightmares that cracked down on northern dreams.

Despite Nash's fear that talking might ruin the privacy of their moment, he asked, "How come today, Dad?"

His father took an extra deep nip. "Aaaaaagh."

Nash waited a long while, long enough to watch a bank of clouds to the east beset the brightness of his morning. Above skeletons of factories that stretched along the Brooklyn riverbank, the clouds weighed themselves like wistful plumes of smoke. Nash sank his face into the cradle of his thick hands, sweating a little, wondering if he should let his question drift, mingle, and disappear into the clouds. Restless, Nash twisted sideways and looked at his father again.

"Dad?"

Justus Ambrose winked at his son and tilted his head to the side. Made a clicking sound like the one that always prodded his horse, Whist Wing, when Justus was in the black cavalry at West Point. Absentmindedly, he chucked Nash under the chin and said, "You're never as tall as when you stoop to help a child."

El niño's roaming knuckles scraped across the roof. Raindrops tapped a restless dance that interfered with slumber. Joana murmured. Nash rushed wide awake, hugging her to his chest. Sleep deprived, they were both weary from fixing up their fixer-upper, at odds for how to spend their first free weekend in two years.

Gently, Nash coaxed Joana onto her right side. Stroked her cheek. Looked into her eyes, which were wide open.

"Nash."

"Baby." He pressed his lips to hers.

She clutched his shoulder. Headlights of a passing car shone on her solitaire diamond, casting the spark of its reflection on her wedding band, dulled metal in absence of the light.

"I don't know if I can do this, Nash. I'm still not *sure*."

Nash propped up his head with an extra pillow. Quickly, ran his hand across the stubble on his head, jaw, and chin.

Slowly, Joana sat up straight and crossed her ankles beneath the white, satin gown she wore. Her thick, black, natural hair looked spongy soft in the half-light of their room.

"I've never tried to get pregnant before. I don't know how to do it."

"Here, let me show you." He beckoned to her. They both laughed.

"Nash, I mean it. What we're thinking about doing is serious. Tell me one more time, how do you *know* it's the right thing—for us?"

"You never used to worry about anything, Baby. Don't start now. We're ready."

"Are we? Can't we just keep doing what we've been doing so perfectly for five years? It's only about three days out of a whole month that we can't...."

"That's not the point anymore, Joa. You'll make a good mother. You're treating me just like a child."

"Would."

"*Would*, what?"

"*Would* make a good mother."

"Then you agree?" He sat up next to her.

"Conditional, not future."

"What do you mean *conditional*?"

"Grammar."

"*Grammar*?"

"Nash, just tell me, why is it so important?"

"Something my father said." He turned on his side, knees pulled toward his chest, covers tugged over his head. Closed his eyes, plunging back toward darkness.

Joana stared hard at his back. If he would just face her again, she would try harder to understand why she was no longer enough for him.

El niño

Nash.

Sometimes, she could say his name to herself and he would hear her. They could be in the same room or miles apart and he was always ready with an answer. Listening to him sleep, deep breaths cycling through his lungs like wind, Joana thought of fathers, never having known her own.

I remember, Nash — what your father said, that day in the park. No one's ever given me a reason.

Agitated, Joana curled into the fetal position on her side of the bed, eyes shut tight. Tiny fists of rain whipped against the windows, building to a tantrum. *El niño* wailed for feeding, refusing desires and regrets, accepting only sleep and dreams.

You can see the head! Bear down, Joana, push!"

The delivery room turned into a box. Joana's feet pushed past the hospital bed, breaking through a wall.

"Just one more good one like that, Joana. Just one more." The voice came from a speaker wedged into a high corner on the yellow wall.

She flutter kicked, trying to shake the baby loose.

"Here they come."

"Twins?"

"In a way."

"The head is out. Shoulders. Torso. It's a girl-boy." The voice was scratchy from a bad connection.

"A girl-boy?"

"Yes, happens roughly every fifty years. Here, hold your baby, Joana." Two immense hands tried to place something in her arms.

Joana screamed. "It's all bloody!"

"What do you expect?"

"Help me clean it up!" She looked around, alone.

"That's your job, as a mother. Here." The hands doubled in size.

"I can't hold it."

"You have to. We're late for lunch."

Voices sound like gargling.

The floor is dirty — black linoleum with specks of dingy white blend with faded gray. I'm sitting in the middle of it. Eight years old. That man who hangs around my mother, he said, "How much longer 'fore she grow up, Nella?" These are the first words I remember anyone ever saying around me.

Joana woke up alone to the sound of a woman's voice, singing, crying, downstairs. When Joana rushed into the kitchen, the large, stainless steel refrigerator door was ajar. The music of the woman's voice louder now.

Love is like a faucet

It turns off and on…

Nash straightened up behind the door, half gallon of milk in his hand.

Joana stood by the black marble island in the center of the kitchen. Took a deep breath and blew it out. "Now, I've done it. I've driven you to Billie."

"Could be worse." Nash poured a glass of milk and held up the container.

Joana shook her head and attempted to laugh. "I'm still getting used to the freezer being on the bottom." She ran her hand along the smooth edge of a black-and-rust speckled counter. "It'll be good to just enjoy this house, you know? Now that it's all finished." She looked around and back at Nash. "We did a good job."

He sipped his milk and closed the refrigerator door. "This has always been a lot of space for just two people."

"All the room we could only dream about, growing up." Joana inched closer to her husband.

Nash shrugged. "I never felt cramped."

"Nash, we haven't had a real vacation since our honeymoon. We've put everything into the house."

He swirled an inch of milk in his glass and emptied it. "Where would you like to go?"

"Someplace warm, soon, before autumn gets too comfortable with itself. It's a *La niña* year. Extra cold."

"Is that where the draft is coming from, Joa?"

"Maybe it's left over from a nightmare." She told him about it.

"I'm sorry about your dream, baby."

"And I'm sorry about yours."

He placed the empty glass of milk on the counter. Considered washing it and changed his mind. "What if you have second thoughts when it's too late, Joa?"

Joana's heartbeat was irregular. "Too late, you mean, to have a child?"

"I'll always love you, Joa. I know that. You know that. I know you love me. This is about something else."

"What, Nash, what *is* it about?"

"Joana, it's a *feeling*. I want to be responsible for someone else—our child. I want to raise a decent human being."

"But look at the world, Nash. It's such a mess!"

"It is what it is, Joa. It can use a lot of help. Things won't get better by themselves."

"I'm still waiting for that feeling, Nash. I really believed it would have rubbed off on me by now. I'm tired of waiting."

"And I can't give up. I'm going back to bed." He walked away.

"Wait." She touched his arm. "Nash, you want to have *my* child?"

"That question, is it another conditional?"

She shook her head. "Present tense."

"All these words, now. I don't know how to answer that one, Joa. I'll sleep on it." He went upstairs.

The stereo was Nash's toy. Joana cupped her ears to muffle the wailing of Billie's voice.

You know, love is like a faucet
It turns off and on....
Sometimes when you think it's on baby
It has turned off and gone....[1]

Joana found the Stop button and pressed it hard, which made her wish she could substitute Rewind, instead.

Nash lay on his back in bed. Knees up. Dick hard. In darkness. He closed his eyes, revisiting the first time he wanted his wife, the first time he made love to her one April, when it was newly spring. He was sitting in his portable, plaid chair on the beach in Alameda one Sunday afternoon, intending to flip through the *New York Times*, but the wind kept turning pages early. One gust tore a headline in two, turning his attention to a school of kiteboarders who rode that same wind across aquamarine water glittered with sunlight. He relaxed fully into the caress of wind and curled his toes beneath the coral sand. Reclining there, he realized why people loved beaches. When the wind was right, beaches brought you home to three elements — earth, water,

---

[1] From *Fine and Mellow*, written and recorded by Billie Holiday.

and air. That day, Joana Carlton, carried by bare feet, provided a fiery fourth. She wore a sky-blue sports bra and white sweat pants. The arms of the matching jacket were tied around the indent of her waist. Her long legs and feet carried her forward gracefully. Joana's hips swayed, slowly keeping time with the water's flow. Her coarse, dark hair was pulled back into a big puff.

A woman like that—that woman—surely had a man, any one she wanted. Maybe, just maybe she was between men like he was between women. Free.

Joana strolled toward Nash. He shaded his eyes from the sun and looked up at her. He liked tall women and she seemed about his height.

"Don't you love all the colors?" He nodded toward the kiteboards.

"Why don't you give it a try?" She put her hands on her hips. Shifted her weight from side to side.

"That just might make me the first brother out there. I don't have to be the first."

She laughed. "I tried it once. Too much work!"

"I know what you mean. Sometimes, it's more fun to play."

"Sometimes. See you." She waved and walked toward the parking lot.

"When?" Nash stood up.

"Maybe next Sunday."

"What if it's a wet one?"

"That won't stop me." She slipped into her jacket.

"Then why, 'maybe'?"

"Depends on you."

It rained the next weekend. Joana ran north as Nash walked south, holding an umbrella, escorting her to her car when she was ready. The next three Sundays were dry, warm, hot. He bought her coffee at a *café* on Park Street in Alameda. She treated him to ice cream near Lake Merritt in Oakland. They held hands and kissed the next time they met.

Midway into their second month, he invited her to spend a weekend with him in Calistoga. She said, "Yes," after he told her there were plenty of vacancies so they could decide about rooms and beds once they arrived. They wound their way through the Napa valley in his fifteen-year-old tan sedan. Seductive signs for wineries enticed them off Highway 29 three times. They stopped to taste *Red Zinfandels*, *Pinot Noirs*, and finally *Merlots* with bittersweet chocolate in St. Helena. Over dinner at the fine corner restaurant on Main Street in Calistoga, Nash asked Joana if she was tired. She shook her head and said, "But I am ready for bed."

Within the hour, they were settled into one cozy room at a bed and breakfast a block away from the restaurant. As Nash slipped the straps of Joana's mauve dress past her shoulders and smoothly ran the tips of his thumbs along her collarbones, she whispered, "Don't worry, I won't get pregnant." He whispered back, "I'm not worried."

The night lightened from charcoal gray to twilight haze. Nash felt his wife get in bed beside him. They both lay on their backs listening to the wind. Sleep was a pretense for him, but he simply could not open his eyes and risk reminders of the present tense. Finally, Nash cleared his throat and spoke.

"We've both been running around so much lately, Baby. How was your week, Joa?"

"We have been running. I found a perfect *T'ai Chi* instructor so now we have seven activities."

Nash counted. "Yoga, Pilates, kick boxing, *capoeira*, aerobics, stretching, and now *Ta'i Chi*."

"I'd like to get something going in the schools, with kids. Maybe we can work on that together." She slipped under his arm and hugged him. "How was your week?"

"This kid came into my office with the usual story, you know, his teacher gave him a choice between the principal and the guidance counselor, and that new principal lost out again. Tell you the truth, Joa, I don't remember details. I just remember saying something I needed to hear."

"What was that?""

Nash opened his eyes. "Don't know where it came from, but I told them there's always a best way to get through any experience. All we have to do is let it come to us and follow it."

Joana looked up at the ceiling, which became a film screen replaying the first night she spent with Nash. His hands had always belonged on her skin because they gave more than they took. She knew she loved him the first Sunday she did not feel compelled to go running—the weekend following Calistoga. After that, he had been the first one to say it, "I love you, Joa." Immediately, she felt that maybe with a man like that—that man—she could learn to love herself.

"Nash."

They turned toward each other. He slid his fingers across the right side of her face, through her hair, letting his hand rest gently at the back of her neck.

"Joana."

He kissed her deeply. Traced her whole body with his hands. She held on to him tightly, pulling him into a place where they both belonged.

"Baby. Baby! BABY!!" He bore down on her, and she pressed him closer. Her ankles were a ribbon tied at the small of his back.

El niño

"Nash, baby, all I need is you...."

El niño toddled into a brand new day, warming up, running toward his sister, careful not to melt her when they finally embraced.

Demonstration

"Bet you twenty dollars it won't fly."

All Charm Palmé had was seventy until payday a week away except he just got fired from a job he never even wanted. Charm didn't have a best friend, he just knew people — like LaNita and DeWayne, coworkers at the local, urban newspaper. It was Friday, their day to eat together at the Chinese restaurant three blocks from their office.

Charm used to desire LaNita, when she talked much less and said a lot more. Now, the girl could force thirty days of conversation into half an hour. She wasn't especially attractive, but he wasn't much to look at, either. He was medium height and wiry while she was taller, thick, and had no waist. Sometimes, he secretly wished they could trade parts of their bodies. Like other women, his name turned her on, and that was good enough for him. Sometimes, there was a kindness to LaNita that still attracted Charm, but whenever he trusted that behavior as her true self, he was disappointed, like now, when once again, she was all too willing to bet against him. DeWayne was just as bad.

"Man, just this once, listen to what everybody knows. People like good news the best when it's happening to them." DeWayne twirled *lo mein* noodles around his chopsticks, one in each hand. His posture curved forward, rounding out his belly.

"That's just because they don't know any better." Charm combed his fork through a mound of shrimp fried rice, resolved to eat it left over, next time he had an appetite.

"What's to know?" LaNita cut the won tons in her soup with a knife and fork. Its savory steam warmed the mid-autumn afternoon.

Charm looked from DeWayne to LaNita. He was twenty-four and they were barely elders at ages thirty and thirty-two. He could not blame them for his decision to get a degree in journalism that was yet to pay a half-month's rent. Neither of them had just fired him for the third-strike typo that ran in the morning's classified section. Certainly, it was not their fault that he had trusted the desperate manager of the advertising department. That man had promised to help him get a shot at working in the news room if Charm would only pick up where his predecessor had left off by quitting on the spot the day Charm turned in his application.

The server who visited their table was an older Asian man of forty years or so. Charm asked him for a box, which arrived immediately. The man carefully transferred Charm's entire meal into the container, right down to the last grain of brown rice. Without being asked, the server packaged the container in a small paper bag and a larger plastic one. He placed the check in front of DeWayne.

Charm put a five-dollar tip on the table and told LaNita, "Forget about that bet. All I need is the right angle for my article."

DeWayne tweezed the last noodle. "All we need is to get back to work on time. They're cracking down all over. Threatening people who've been there for ten and twenty years if they're a minute late." He looked at his watch. "I've got my regular appointment at the barber shop—5:30 sharp."

Smoothing out the tip he left, Charm said, "They let me go, today."

LaNita shook her head and winced. For the first time, she picked up the check and paid it.

"I thought you saved your boss' butt when what-'is-name quit on him that day." DeWayne shuttled a bottle of soy sauce back and forth between his hands.

"It's my spelling. I've made some pretty bad typos."

"Like what?" LaNita wanted to know.

"*Hose for sale, $475,000; altering wheels* instead of *all-terrain* for this truck; then somebody was having an estate sale; I typed *escape*."

"Yeah, brother. Those are some pretty bad mistakes." LaNita couldn't help it. She started to laugh. DeWayne tried to control himself, but he joined her. Outnumbered, Charm shook his head and smiled.

"I can spell, it's just when I'm writing anything, even those stupid ads, I don't think about editing. We get paid—I *got* paid—commissions based on selling the most ads. Sometimes, maybe most of the time, I forgot to check my spelling before the ads ran. I didn't have the time."

Standing, LaNita said, "I'll make sure human resources does right by you, Charm. Want me to try and find you something else?"

"If you see something, let me know. Thanks, Nita."

DeWayne got to his feet. "I'll put in a good word for you too, man." Nervously, he checked his watch and said, "Damn. I got to go." He went.

LaNita looked like she wanted to say something. If Charm had to guess, he'd say it was something like, "I hate to leave you here like this." But for once, she let her eyes do the talking. All they said was, "Sorry," in ten different ways before she sauntered toward the creaky wooden door.

Demonstration

The server placed a hot pot of tea in front of Charm's folded hands and said, "Before, I forgot."

When Charm said, "Thank you," he believed the server knew those words applied to much more than a steeping cup of jasmine tea.

The people needed that presidential candidate to win so badly that they formed a thick strand around the urban courthouse on a seasonable Sunday afternoon. The white-and-green building functioned with minimal attention to design. Its presence as a landmark was capriciously reinforced by a manmade lake, an art museum and a newly retrofitted library.

It was two days after Charm got fired, two days before the general election. Most impressive about this demonstration of desire were the threads of silence that imposed uncommon order on a community that could otherwise have been a mob. Journalists in the city thought nothing of this gathering that drew outside the box of statistics tied to drugs, violence, and corruption. To them, there was no story here. But Charm Palmé was not a journalist. Then and there, he claimed himself as a news reporter.

Keeping his place in line, waiting to be counted with all the other early, watchful voters, Charm wondered if this movement was new or whether it was *status quo* waiting to be named. Answers to the Five W's were obvious—Who? What? When? Where? Why? Could there be a sixth? *Was* there another way to tell a story and make it seem like news?

Infiltrated by cautious voices, the line flowed slowly like fog across the bay.

"He's got to win."

"He will. He will."

"I'm just afraid...."

"Afraid of what?"

"He won't make it."

"You mean...."

"Someone could get to him. He could get stopped."

"No one's ever had more security."

"We'll see how well it works."

Charm turned around and looked into the young faces of two white people. The woman had faraway looks in her charcoal-grey eyes as if she had traveled too much, too far, too soon. The man possessed the earthbound solidity of someone who knew things without having to discover them.

"So, you think he's gonna win?" Charm was careful to ask both of them, wanting to appear unbiased.

"Yes," he said.

She said, "No."

The man stared hard at the woman as if she belonged with someone else.

"Then, what are you doing here?"

"I can't say."

"You don't know?"

"I just can't say." She dropped out of the line exactly when the entrance to the building was in easy sight.

The man squinted as he watched the woman walk away. "You think you know someone."

All Charm could say was, "I don't understand it." Halfway up the ramp, he felt closer to his story. Step by step, Charm was elevated on the ladder of history.

Was? Was this not the very landmark where, forty years ago, the community assembled to demonstrate their faith, their hopes, their dreams?

Demonstration

Then, the demonstrators were largely black, assembled to win fair treatment of a black man imprisoned for a crime that had been committed.

Were? Now, the "demonstrators" were mixed, assembled to win fair treatment of a black man running for *precedent.*

As Charm entered the side door of the courthouse, the black police and white security guards could not have been more courteous. Frantically, he patted the inner pockets of his blue, flannel shirt—the outer ones of his green, corduroy car coat, searching for the tools of his neglected trade. He packed no piece of paper. He could not find a pen. Memory agreed to serve.

Cross Country

The speed of darkness cast heavy shadows everywhere and raced as equal partner to the wind. Distant bulbs of light testified to fleeting towns, introspective like private thoughts, unsafe. Only a train—clinking, clanging, rattling its news along endless miles of hammered tracks—could tolerate this tone of black. Only a train of thought could chase the tails of days cross country.

Wide awake in her sleeping car, Merina Jordan lost all sense of time and place. If only she could as easily displace her memories of two recent men—Carter Hathaway and Daví Almeida.

Café Radio was on a quiet corner across from Thompkins Square Park in the East Village, which would always be the Lower East Side of Manhattan to Merina. Shortly after finishing college in the city, she migrated less than one mile from the projects to a brownstone on West 4th Street near the Waverly theater. A dozen years ago, already, making her too old to be young and too young to be old. In that time, brick-faced tenements were powdered over by smooth façades. High-rise co-ops stamped out vacant lots of weeds. A swimming pool hid behind a black-barred fence like a child thinly protected by their mother's faded skirt. There was no hiding from the projects, which lay beyond Ave. D—the final lettered street—whose fissured asphalt ran parallel to the sewage-treated East River. The projects loomed tall like Goliath, slinging shadows that contested any evidence of light.

Like a salmon retracing the arc of its existence, Merina revisited *Café Radio* each Saturday afternoon. In the summer, when grenades of humidity bloated everything and everyone it touched, she preceded those visits with a swim in her old neighborhood. The rest of the week, walking kept Merina fit, but she still felt flabby in her gray, ribbed tank top. Her maroon, too-short cotton exercise pants were rolled up to just below her knees to make the deficiency in length less obvious.

It was early July and instead of finding two lifeguards and more kids than open water at the small 10th Street pool, a rude *Out of Order* sign met Merina at the rusting gate. She pushed her polarized sunglasses past her hairline to make sure she was seeing straight. All along the street, open manholes were cordoned off and topped by awkward plastic tubes that spouted plumes of stifling, smelly steam. These monuments to construction thinned out by the time Merina reached the *bodega* on Ave. B and 10th St., where she always bought the Saturday edition of the Sunday paper.

"Sorry, *amiga*." Manny, the brown-skinned man with the pock-marked face was around her age. Stocky like a heavy bag. "The paper, it's not here yet. For you, the next one, it's free." He stepped from behind the counter and went over to one of the racks. Handed Merina a pack of gum. "Here. This, it's for you."

"That's okay, *amigo*. It's not your fault." Merina tried to return the gum.

"*Por favor*. Please." He placed the gum in her hand. A male customer came in and Manny swiftly returned to the cash register.

Merina regarded the peppermint gift—six pieces of bubble gum. She peeled off a wrapper, bit into the first pink cube, and chewed. The gum was soft, its juice too sweet.

"*Gracias, eh?*"

"You're welcome. Aren't you gonna blow some bubbles?"

"I have to practice. It's been a while."

"See you next week, *amiga.*"

Manny smiled. Had that always been his custom? She almost told him about her upcoming trip cross country to visit Sandrine, her best friend since childhood. Thinking better of it, she kept that business to herself.

Inside *Café Radio*, jazz improvised from two tiny speakers perched on shelves above a doorway that led to the kitchen. A wooden ceiling fan cut through air like dull scissors snipping away at a paper bag. Merina read the large sandwich board on the wall behind the counter where a woman with long, wavy red hair and freckles fixed food and drinks. Seemed like somebody different was working there every single week and the menu changed more often than the weather.

"Hi. Could I have an organic chai *latte*?" Merina looked at the black-faced clock with white numbers and hands whose ticking was out of sync with the ceiling fan. It was only two o'clock. "Would you make that a large?"

"We're out of the organic."

"Out of the organic." Merina looked at the sandwich board and chose a matcha green tea *latte* with nonfat milk.

"Hot?" With her striped short sleeve, the woman wiped beads of sweat from her forehead.

Merina nodded.

Pressing a button on the cash register, the woman said, "Four dollars."

Watching her own hand count each bill, Merina was awed by this expensive transaction.

"I give you this and you'll give me a hot cup of water with a splash of milk and some kind of sweetened, colored powder."

The woman nodded. "Twelve whole ounces. I'll bring it to you."

Three girls, high-school age, were sitting at Merina's usual round table in the far corner. The black girl was outnumbered by two white companions and she seemed more at ease than Merina had ever felt in that same seat. Empty, square tables surrounded the mixture of girls, but Merina chose the one farthest away, to the right of the front door, in the window. Her new table was tall, circled by three pine chairs with rigid backs. She placed her quilted, pale orange tote bag on the seat to her right and sat in the stool next to it. Rearranged her dark-brown, spring-tight hair, which covered the nape of her neck and barely fit into the yellow swimming cap folded neatly inside her bag.

Outside the window, the four street corners formed one of many intersections on *Loaisada* and in Alphabet City, new names Merina rejected that were oblivious of her past. She took off her sunglasses and placed them on the table, noticing that a vine of red tulips was painted along its square edges. A small, copper, wire basket to her right held a stack of brown napkins and wooden coffee stirrers. Long flower boxes crowded with red geraniums, fragrant lavatera, and orange marigolds sat on the sidewalk at either side of the door. On the closest corner, clumsy flies patrolled mounds of trash that belched beyond a cluster of aluminum garbage cans.

Pulling herself closer to the table, Merina watched joggers turn into runners the closer they got to the projects. She knew they would be sprinting by the time they reached "The Circle," one block from East River Park. Though she had moved from her neighborhood, escape was never her desire. Monday through Friday, September through June, Merina returned to the light-blue-brick building that she swore remembered her very first day of school. She was expected there to run her reading program, which she created for every child who crossed over to the distant shore of Ave. D.

Café Radio used to be a record store. Merina could still picture it the day she bought her first album there: "California Dreamin'." She had just read an article about San Francisco's cable cars in *National Geographic*, inhaling all of the golden photographs. That scene had embellished itself considerably over the years. So, when Sandrine upped, moved, and invited Merina to visit her in Los Angeles, the calling was expected, the timing suitable, and the impending escape a thrill.

People were streaming into the *café* now, crowding the cash register, their voices scoring over jazz with noise.

My drink should be ready.

Merina twisted toward the counter. She waved, winked, and nodded, trying to get the redhead's attention. Opting for patience, she replaced her chewed-out gum with a fresh piece and blew her first bubble in years.

"I hope this is yours."

The man who spoke was at least two heads taller than Merina from where she sat on her stool. One of his hands was slipped inside a khaki pants pocket while the other held a clear glass by its thin handle. The top button of his blue, short-sleeved shirt was undone, revealing smooth skin — dark brown, a shade or two deeper than her own. Each foot was perfectly centered in two *terra cotta* floor tiles as if their sole purpose was to frame the outlines of his feet.

"Mind if I set this down? It's hot."

Merina reigned in her bubble. "You don't work here."

"Uh, uh. But I did see you sitting in the window when I came in. I asked the server what you were drinking."

She laughed. "Oh, kind of like we're in a bar."

"Something like that." He placed the glass beside her on the table. "Would you mind if I grabbed that empty stool next to you, at least while I wait for my iced coffee?"

Few men Merina had known were that easy on her eyes. Three more days and she would be on her way to California. She pretended this man was a passenger who would come and go like any travel destination.

She said, "I don't mind," and he sat down.

Merina reached for a napkin and disposed of her gum. "Iced coffee, huh?"

"Yeah, I like to keep things cool, you know?"

Merina nodded and sipped her *latte*. She was a bit startled that it tasted green. "I read somewhere that drinking something hot, in heat, cools you down."

He wiped his forehead. "Let me know about that, will you?"

The redhead brought his iced coffee and smiled it right in front of him. She took her time returning to the counter.

Merina shook her head. "I might still be waiting on mine if you didn't come along." With her left hand, she lifted her glass toward him. "Thank you."

He held up his drink to toast. "You're welcome, Southpaw. My name's Carter Hathaway."

They shared a nod and he kept talking.

"Listen, I just started working in the neighborhood, right up the street, there, at the Boys Club. I'm from Brooklyn."

"Brooklyn!? A traveler."

Carter smiled. "I *think* I know what you mean. Listen, if I give you my business card, will you tell me your name?"

He produced the card. She read it, tapped it on the table a few times and said, "Me-ri-na Jor-dan. You're working on a Saturday, Carter?"

"I like having the whole building to myself so I can think. A lot goes on in the summer, Merina — day camp with all kinds of activities. Tennis, pool, all the ball games, track, gymnastics. Name it. Lots of field trips plus a sleep-away program. Nice clean pool. Matter of fact, a new swimming session starts next week." He took a sip of his coffee, wiped his neat mustache and laughed.

"What?"

"It might seem out of line."

Merina shrugged. "We're both grown." She popped another piece of gum in her mouth and blew a big bubble, which he popped gently with a coffee stirrer. They both laughed.

He shook his head. "Last thing I want to do is offend you, Merina."

"Want me to guess?"

"I'm not one to play games."

"Alright. Just tell me." She relaxed into her chair.

Carter rested an elbow on the table and looked directly at Merina. "For years, they've made the kids swim naked. All boys, mind you, but still."

"Still, what?"

"I don't feel right asking the fellas to do something I wouldn't do."

"You a swimmer, Carter?"

"Yeah. You?"

Merina nodded. "Can I see how big it is?"

Carter sat up straight. "Beg pardon?"

"The pool, Carter."

They snickered, chuckled, and laughed loud enough to turn heads.

"Want to get out of here before they ask us to leave?" He stood up and took a few steps to the front door, which was wide open. A mild breeze stirred on the sidewalk as an ice cream cart jingled toward the park. "Can I get you a popsicle, Merina? A cone, maybe?"

Merina collected her belongings. Stood beside Carter at the threshold and looked into his eyes. They were black and shiny like brand new marbles. "Want to know my favorite summer treat, Carter?"

"Tell me." He spoke softly.

"A *coco*," she whispered.

He nodded. "Those smooth, sweet icies guys sell in their green, wooden carts?"

"Um hmm." Merina nodded.

"I'm a *piragua* man, myself. I love to watch them shave that ice — the anticipation of it on a day just like this, you know?"

"You did say you like to keep things cool. What flavor?"

"Wild cherry."

Merina frowned. "All that dye — it turns your tongue red."

Carter quickly stuck out his tongue and drew it back inside his mouth. "It's worth the mess."

Merina touched his arm. "Let's go."

"Where to?"

She nodded toward the park. "If we're lucky, we'll both get our wish."

The building where Carter worked was three stories tall of yellow brick. Merina would have guessed that it was only two, and it had always seemed smaller the countless times she rushed past it to and from work, year after year, autumn following summer, winter catching up with spring. Standing at the bottom step of its upswept entrance, Merina visualized the swimming pool.

"There's something I've been wanting to ask you, Merina, before it's too late."

Carter's voice was sudden after he and Merina had shared silent smiles while strolling through the crowded park. A free, loud concert made it hard to talk and listen. Their discovery of a *coco* man and a *piragua* woman operating side by side seemed like some kind of omen, neither Merina nor Carter venturing what type.

"Listen, Merina…could I taste your *coco*?"

She peered into her white paper cup with its neat, vertical folds. "You don't expect me to let you finish it, do you? That's always the best part—finishing."

"I like the beginning and middle just as much. Here." He handed her the white cone of his cherry *piragua*. "Can we trade?"

"Let me see your tongue."

He obliged, revealing red evidence.

"Alright. Okay. I'll do this, just to keep you company." She looked longingly at her cup, which held around a heaping tablespoon of softened *coco*. Quickly, she exchanged it for the small pool of red ice waiting for her in the tip of his cone. They tilted back their heads, let the dregs slide down their throats, and tossed the containers in a trash can at the corner.

"So, Merina, do you still want to see how big it is?"

She looked at the building. "The pool?"

"The pool." He extended his hand and she took it.

Afternoon sunlight billowed through clerestory windows, brightening seven lanes of aqua water. Merina counted them while walking along the edge of the pool. She reached the deep end and stopped there, at thirteen feet, bathed by chlorine silence.

Carter stood beside her. "How'd you learn to swim?"

"I jumped right in." She looked at the water, reading her thoughts into its depth. *I'll be on a train in three days.*

Merina turned toward him. "Carter, is anyone else here?"

He shook his head.

She let her tote bag fall to the floor and smiled at him. "I've got a swimsuit in there, but you know what?"

Carter looked at the bag, then at her. "Girl, are you *serious*?"

She took off her maroon exercise pants. Her gray tank top. Matching panties and camisole, powder blue. Jumped into the pool and freestyled toward the other end. The water warmed, inch by inch, and by the time she reached the wall, Merina felt like she was sweating. To cool down, she stretched her arms straight above her head and pushed off into a slow, rhythmic back stroke. Her body rotated from side to side as she glided through the water, propelled by perfect flutter kicks and windmill arms. Under the blue and white triangular flags yards from the opposite wall, she prepared to turn around. Flipping, her feet brushed Carter's thighs. Beside him, she started treading water.

Carter held tightly to the side of the pool with one hand. He placed the other lightly on Merina's shoulder. "Merina, tell me—what is it you want me to do?"

"Swim with me." She took off in a model breast stroke.

Carter swam a rapid freestyle past her. Waited for her at the other end, winded. Merina's breath was even.

"It's been a while, Merina."

"Swim *with* me, Carter."

They freestyled together. Smoothly, Merina alternated breathing on each side every three strokes while Carter gulped air when his right arm rose straight, tense, and high out of the water, again and again, wasting precious energy.

At the wall, treading water more easily than before, Merina waited for him to catch his breath.

"Listen, Merina, is this all you want to do — swim?"

"You did it, Carter."

"Did what?"

"Something you wouldn't ask the boys to do."

"I thought I had a reason."

"Are you still going to change the rule, now that you've done it and see how good it feels — how *free*?"

"But Merina, this doesn't feel good at all. I thought I had a reason."

She swam away from him and left the pool. Merina Jordan dried off, dressed swiftly, and waved goodbye. At the double blue doors beneath the Exit sign, she took one last look at the pool. It was big — and beautiful, too.

The train panted into the Chicago station like a stray dog hunting shelter. Two more days to San Francisco and Sandrine, who had moved there six weeks ago to find her man and settle down.

Merina closed her eyes and tried to doze off in the sudden stillness. She imagined this new darkness as deep water that made it easier to float and drift than crawling on the surface. A loud wake interrupted—an announcement that the train would be delayed for at least one hour. Was she supposed to stay put for all that extra time? Merina's body gave her little trouble in that regard but her mind would not be tamed. Insistently, it heaped up scattered thoughts about Daví.

Sale!

A great big sign took up half the window of a small sporting goods shop on West 8th Street off Avenue of the Americas. It was a sunny, Sunday afternoon. Merina wore a velour, cranberry skirt and a gauze, turquoise blouse to celebrate the brightness of the day. The shop was five short blocks from her apartment and she had never been inside. Passing the entrance, a color caught her eye—orange-yellow like a Pacific sunset. From the sidewalk, the item looked like a simple, sleeveless blouse. At the threshold of the shop, it turned out to be a one-piece swimsuit with delicately braided straps that criss-crossed in a low-cut back. In her hands, it promised to be a perfect fit and the suit felt like second skin. The sale price was seventy-five dollars, which failed Merina's standard for a bargain. Walking around the store, she weighed the potential of buyer's remorse against willpower at the threshold of the dressing room.

"That color is perfect with your complexion."

She turned around and faced a tall white man with shiny, dark hair pulled back into a short pony tail. His cobalt blue eyes were feral, stirring the impulse of fight or flight.

"What would you know about my skin?"

"It is beautiful."

"What exactly are you shopping for?"

The man's face turned coral as he laughed.

Merina placed the suit on a rack that happened to be empty. The man quickly glimpsed the tag on the garment and said, "Perhaps you think it is too expensive." He leaned against a wall, folded his arms and relaxed. "What if you miss this opportunity?"

A short, shapeless woman came along and read aloud the sign that said, "Four items allowed." She had three and grabbed the swimsuit. Before she could mutter, "Where's the attendant?," a tall, thin, black woman with thick, brown, wiry hair appeared and gave the customer a number 4.

Merina watched the woman nervously disappear beside a scuffed, white wall of the dressing room with *her* suit, convinced that this adversary was too short, too wide — her skin too pale to carry such bright color.

The man whispered to Merina, "You're just going to let that happen?"

Merina ignored him though she did approach the attendant and asked, "Have a lot of people tried on that swimsuit?"

"That funny orange one?"

"*Funny?*"

"If it was up to me, I'd give that thing away." The attendant waved her hand as if littering.

"Do you think that woman in there will buy it?" Merina's tone was accusatory.

The attendant shook her head, rattling a pair of large, gold hoop earrings that circled her full, brown cheeks.

"Why not?" Merina asked.

"It won't fit right. That color's too large for her."

The woman emerged from the dressing room and threw the suit on the counter in front of the attendant. Merina snatched up the garment and darted to the checkout stand where she searched for her wallet and came up empty handed.

"I have to get the money." Merina clutched the suit. "Would you hold it for me? I'll be back in thirty minutes."

A blank look filled the cashier's pale gray eyes. "We close in ten, but it'll be here when you come back, tomorrow."

"How do you know?"

The cashier shrugged. "The style's nice but that color."

Merina felt crazed and tried to regain some composure. "I meant how do you know I'll be back?"

Looking at the clock, the cashier said, "Wishful thinking. I'm tired of looking at that thing."

A line of procrastinating shoppers was thickening behind Merina. She stepped aside. The cashier and a male security guard reminded her to surrender the suit. Merina did this with a combination of resentment and relief.

At the northeast corner of West 8th and Avenue of the Americas, Merina tapped her left foot to the time of the traffic signal as it slowly counted down from 13, to 12, to 10. As those seconds mingled with the humidity, Merina tried to talk herself out of wanting the blasted bathing suit, which was so cool. It wasn't the suit, it was the color.

Finally, red turned to green. She crossed the street and stepped up onto the curb. The blue leather of her sandals against the gray sidewalk made it look cleaner than it was. Merina had no favorite color since childhood. In the winter, when all the trees were bare, sunrise orange shined through her seventh-floor window in the projects overlooking the East River. Thinking of that room now, she wondered if anyone was home.

"This belongs to you."

Merina looked to her left. The white man from the shop held up the suit as if it were the cape of a matador. In waning daylight, he appeared to be around her age. The street was crowded, people charging all around. Seeing the color again made her dizzy. Against her better judgment, she answered him even though there was no question.

"That's just not true."

"What would you say if I told you I owned that store?"

She tilted her head to one side. "Do you?"

"I do not."

Merina smiled. "You like to play games."

"Don't you? They can be a lot of fun." He tried to put the suit in her hands, but she kept walking, faster than before. He kept up.

"This would look very bad on me." The man held it up in front of his torso.

Merina imagined the figure of another woman in the suit and said, "Something tells me you wouldn't let it go to waste."

"So, you do like to play games. Why don't you just ask me if I'm...attached to somebody?"

"Because I don't care."

He held up his left hand anyway. His ring finger was bare.

Merina stared at him. "Now, there's some solid proof."

They both laughed as he put his left hand in his left pocket and squeezed the swimsuit with his right.

"What were you doing in that store?" Merina stood back and folded her arms.

"I saw the Sale! sign. What's the point of going in a store if you don't buy something?"

"Right," she said thinking, *I can't let him follow me home.* "Tell you what, I'll buy the swimsuit from you. If you'll give me an address, I promise I'll send you a money order tomorrow morning."

He gave her the suit. "You could just come to my *café*." His left hand reappeared. "Here. You're the first one to have one of my new cards. My *café*, it's just a few blocks away."

Merina took the card and put it in her teal, *faux* suede shoulder bag. "Don't worry, I'll get you your money."

"Don't *you* worry. I won't follow you."

Good for his word, he stole away.

Carnaval. The swimsuit's official color replaced the Pacific sunset, which had lost its grip on the horizon.

Carnaval. It seemed the suit should be at least two colors to have a name like that. Confident that it would fit, at the foot of the spiral staircase in her loft, Merina put the suit in the washer with a small load of clothes she had set aside for her trip. Her green, leather wallet was on the kitchen counter. She put it in her shoulder bag, took out the man's card and read the white, cursive letters embossed on a black background:

Daví João Almeida, Proprietor

Saudades

609 Waverly Place

Manhattan

212-555-0110

Get it over with, Merina told herself. *See that white man one more time to pay.*

On Waverly Place, the numbers jumped from 607 to 611. Merina walked back and forth between those addresses several times before noticing a courtyard. Approaching it, she discovered an entrance that was sheltered by ivy and led to the brick façade of 609. Standing at this opening, Merina wondered how many times she had passed it by simply because she had no prior reason to acknowledge its existence. Eyes disguised as windows in apartments and offices all along that block stared at her through dusk. For a split second, it felt natural to be watched while watching more carefully than before, but as seconds built toward minutes, that fleeting rhythm gave way to impatience. Merina only wore a watch on weekdays, but she set her internal clock to get in and out of 609 in under ten minutes.

Yellow walls inside *Saudades* electrified the place like midnight sun. People waited for tables, some on foot, others sitting, while a short, *ethnic*, hostess with long, shapely legs poured red wine into any glass extended. Merina approached her.

"Pardon me."

"Here, have some *Chianti Clásico*." The glass appeared to fill itself.

"Thank you, but I'm not here for dinner. I just need sixty seconds with the owner."

"That would be a first."

"How's that?"

"Let me just say he's not someone who can be rushed. He's expecting you?"

"Could you just tell him the woman with the...from the store is here—the sporting goods store on West 8th?" Merina showed the business card to the hostess and claimed the glass of *Chianti*. "Here, let me pay you." She reached inside her shoulder bag.

The hostess shook her head. "On the house." She was studying the card. "I'll be damned."

"What?"

The hostess stared directly at her. "I never knew he had a middle name." She returned the card to Merina. "I haven't seen him today, but you can try his office. Straight back, past the kitchen. Make a left at the restroom. It's the sage door at the end of the hall."

"Sage?"

"He just had the whole place painted." The hostess excused herself and sat a group of four who had been waiting.

Merina could not get past the spicy smells rushing from the kitchen. They tagged her and sent her back to summers filled with ice cream trucks, jumping rope and picnics at the beach. A rotund, handsome chef smiled and placed a small, square pastry in ribbed white paper in her palm. Merina took a bite and closed her eyes. The flavors were familiar, but harder to pin down than ideal weather. What would you call that? What would you…?

Merina did not realize that she was speaking until the chef replied, "*Saudades.*"

Slowly, she opened her eyes and said the word, "*Saudades.*" She took a sip of wine. "Oh! Sorry! They probably aren't supposed to go together, but they do. They do."

"Yes, they do."

Merina finished the pastry. She crumbled the paper and the chef offered his hand as a disposal.

"That was divine. Thank you."

The chef nodded politely and returned to his work.

At the end of the hall around the corner from the kitchen, the sage door glowed, sandwiched between two blue-gray walls. Merina felt anxious about the time. More than ten minutes had passed and she wanted to keep her promise to herself. So, she reset her internal clock for another ten, charged toward the door and knocked hard, just short of pounding.

Daví opened up. Three simple colors defined him—black silk slacks and a matching shirt, coral skin, blue eyes. No jewelry, not even a watch.

"Ah, if only you would tell me your name."

Merina detected an accent that was feather light. Had it escaped her earlier, or did he turn it on especially for her?

He leaned toward her glass, closed his eyes, and breathed in deeply. "Mmm, our very best—the *Chianti Clásico*. I was just about to pour some for myself. Come, join me. Please."

He walked toward an oak wine rack posed against a far wall. The room was small, but so tidy it felt spacious. A rectangular, glass desk was the exact length of a long, narrow window that traveled the length of the wall directly behind the throne-like, green brocade chair. Merina's eyes tasted the colors as toppings to *Saudades*—cranberry carpet, lime-green walls, *meringue* shades of Tiffany floor lamps in three corners. She finished her wine and looked for a place to put her empty glass. He took it from her, filled the glass, and drank.

"I've had enough." Merina took out her wallet. "Twenty, forty, sixty, seventy-five." She placed the bills on his desk.

"Hmm." Daví stroked the smoothness of his chin.

"What?"

"This does not include the tax."

"Let me see the receipt."

He opened a desk drawer and produced it. "I kept it as a souvenir."

Merina looked at the piece of paper, rechecked her wallet, and neatly piled the balance on top of the companion dollars.

"There you are, Daví. Exact change."

"Finally, you have said my name, now tell me yours."

"You don't need to know."

"Now, how could you know what I need?"

"It doesn't matter."

"What I need matters very much. We are talking about your name and that matters to me."

She meant to start walking, say nothing, but the question, "Why?," escaped from her betraying mouth.

"I was raised to use good manners. Why should I be so rude for no good reason?"

Merina thought about the clean swimsuit inside her washer. *This is a business transaction*, she told herself. *I'm not selling my name.*

She faced Daví and gave him what he asked for.

He repeated her name, *Merina,* with that disarming accent before selecting a bottle from the wine rack. "Are you sure you will not have some more? Wine is the only thing I choose by the label. Look at this one."

"I have to go." She turned toward the glowing sage door. It loomed like a mirage and she could not move her feet.

He showed her the bottle. The label was a circle, a lettered maze. Black italic print on a white background spelling out *Saudades.*

"You do know what it means, Merina."

She stepped back and recited, "*Almeida. Saudades.* Portuguese words. I'll look up *saudades.*"

Daví said, "I will tell you what it means, why it is the name of this place." He made a sweeping motion with his left hand then pressed his palms together. "Something is always missing, Merina. I want people to come here and find it, whatever it is."

"But after that, won't something else be missing?"

He laughed. "Exactly! So that will keep them coming back!"

At once, she felt the two of them were not alone. She noticed a small, sepia photograph on his desk. From an angle, she was able to make out the subjects: an attractive dark man who looked black beside a pretty woman who appeared white. Their perfect pose could not conceal a certain distance from life and one another. The woman faded from Merina's vision, but the man's face became more familiar.

"Almeida. Paulo Almeida, the soccer player. Your father?"

"And my mother. You are surprised?"

"I don't know you, so everything is a surprise."

"You follow sports?"

She shook her head. "My parents. I've never been a fan of rules."

Daví took one step closer to her. "Every game has them, sooner or later." He cupped a hand to his ear, closed his eyes, and smiled. "Hear that?"

Merina listened carefully, hearing tribal drums and rippling bells between heartbeats.

"The musicians are here. Late as usual. If they were on time, something would be wrong. Let us go." He walked past her and opened the door where she joined him at the threshold. Daví placed his hand on the middle of Merina's back. He was close enough that she could smell *Saudades*. Against her better judgment, she turned, slightly. His hand traveled to her shoulder. She looked directly at him—his eyes, ultramarine, set into the coral of his face, surrounded by his black hair, which was an outline against the glowing, sage door.

"You don't seem *real*." She placed her hand on his forearm.

He looked at her bare, brown fingers on his smooth, black sleeve. A dimple in Daví's right cheek deepened his smile. "You noticed?"

"So, we're both left handed." Merina laced her fingers tightly behind her back and nodded toward the door. "Aren't you going to close it?"

He looked at his office and back at her. "I want to leave it open."

They shared the hallway, walking side by side, until they arrived at the kitchen where Merina stopped.

"What's in those *Saudades*, Daví?"

The chef looked up from his long, metal preparation table. Daví winked at him, then at Merina and whispered, "Secrets."

When they reached the edge of a small dance floor, he took her hands and started dancing. It had been ages, but soon Merina's feet befriended the *Samba*. Before long, sweat separated their hands and watered the rest of their bodies. The band played one continuous song that emptied every seat. Servers refilled pitchers of icy lemon water on each table and reserved one for Daví and Merina at the bar. Food got cold and was happily reheated until the band, exhausted, simply had to end the set.

After an embracing round of applause for the musicians, Merina and Daví joined the others outside in the courtyard where the air was cool and jasmine sweet.

"Most nights, I go for a walk right about now, Merina."

"Where to?"

"*Noirée* for *crèpes*."

Her stomach growled. She spoke quickly to muffle its noise.

"*Noirée*?"

"You know it, Merina?"

"I know...."

"*...noire* is French for black." They both knew.

"I can guess what *noirée* means."

"Why guess? You can ask Elena, the owner. Come." He held out his hand.

"I can't hold your hand, Daví."

"I move too fast for you?"

"I just can't."

"Like you 'couldn't' tell me your name?"

"No. This time there's nothing you can say or do that will change my mind."

Moving beside him along the humid, busy, late-night street, Merina sensed the comfort Daví felt with himself and wondered what it would take to absorb that kind of confidence—it fell outside the darkness of her reach. She knew many women would be happy for a one-night stand with him, ecstatic at the prospect of a second, delirious at the possibility of a relationship—white women and many a *noirée*. If she wanted to, she could touch him and he would respond, and so would she—but how?

They walked through Washington Square Park, drifting past those who could not sleep, those who slept by day, those whose dogs demanded hydrants in the middle of the night. Stopped at a red traffic light, Daví asked, "Why did you come out with me, Merina?"

"Hunger. My treat."

The light turned green. Soon, they were sitting at a round, metal table on the sidewalk outside *Noirée*. Small, round lanterns—light blue, orange, pink, and sage—were strung along the tops of windows. The little globes cast a dreamlike luminance across the patina of the table where Merina sat uneasily across from Daví. Of ten tables, three others were taken, all by couples in arrayed states of happiness.

Soon, a stately, tan-skinned woman with long, platinum-gray hair appeared dressed in a sleeveless midnight blue dress that barely hid her knees. She held an amber-colored glass plate topped with a *crèpe* that oozed dark berries from each end, bathed in streams of sweet cream. The dish glowed at the cosmic center of the colored lanterns.

"Daví! Right on time as always. Perhaps you're in the mood for something different tonight." The woman set the plate in the middle of the table. She glanced at Merina and ran her fingers through Daví's thick hair. He caught her roaming hand and kissed the red polish on her fingertips.

"Merina I-do-not-know-your-last-name, meet Elena Noirée."

Merina looked from Elena to Daví. "Any reason you didn't tell me it was a family name? Is everything a game to you, Daví?"

"No." He smiled and shook his head.

Addressing Elena, Merina asked, "What does your last name mean?"

Elena shrugged. "What does *your* last name mean, Merina?"

"I don't know. It doesn't draw attention."

Daví raised his hand and said, "Teacher, I know what my last name means. It has an Arabic root—*al medina* for "the city," which one, I don't know."

"Don't let your *crèpe* get cold." Elena gathered her hair behind her shoulders and disappeared inside the *café*.

Daví turned to the side and crossed his leg. "So, you don't like to draw attention, Merina?"

"I don't like feeling outnumbered."

"Now that we are one on one, let's do what we came here to do— eat." Daví offered his fork to Merina and nodded toward the *crèpe*. "Taste it. Tell me what you think."

Using her own utensils, she cut a piece and sampled. Merina rarely consumed sweets or drank wine. The subtle sugars from the *Chianti*, the chef's *Saudade*, and Elena's *crêpe* were temptations that intruded on her system. No longer hungry, after just one bite, she concluded, "I like the *Saudades* better."

"Let me see if I agree with you." Using his spoon, he scooped a big bite into his mouth then wiped his coral lips perfectly clean with a cloth, saffron napkin. "*Saudades, crêpes, noirée, Merina* — I am trying to decide — do we put too much weight on words and names, or do we take them for granted?"

"There is no *we*. I take names and words quite seriously, Daví." She could not stop herself from thinking, *Who is he*?

Daví leaned forward and folded both arms on the table. "There is something I must say to you, Merina."

"*Must?*" The aftertaste of that word reduced the *crêpe* to dust.

"Some time, Merina, I would like to spend the night with you. More than that."

"That could never happen." She pushed the plate away.

"Because you are black and I look white? They are just colors like your turquoise blouse and cranberry skirt that is the same shade as the carpet in my office — the bathing suit."

"It can be that simple for you, Daví. We both know what people do to carpets." She folded her hands on the table. "There are just too many things you could never understand about me."

"You have never...had a *relationship*...with a white man?"

She looked directly at him. "That's none of your business!"

"I am just wondering how you can be so sure about what I can and cannot understand. Your black lovers, they have all understood you?"

"We've understood things that never needed explanations."

"Like what?"

"They're like *Saudades* — missing parts that almost make us whole."

He leaned closer to her. Merina pressed into the back of her chair.

"You are the most beautiful woman I have ever seen, Merina. *Verdade*."

"*Verdade?*"

"The truth."

Merina's face grew warm. Different men had called her *pretty*. *Beautiful* was a foreign word it would take practice to accept. She blurted out a, "Thank you," then asked, "How do you say *blue* in Portuguese?"

"*Azul.*"

"*Azul.* Your eyes. They're used to getting what they want, aren't they?"

"Sometimes."

Elena replaced the half-eaten *crêpe* with a fresh pot of decaf that smelled like cinnamon, licorice, and mint. She unloaded a copper colored tray that held two brown-and-white cups, a pair of miniature spoons, and a stainless-steel creamer. A gray cat led her to the sidewalk where they both watched the nocturnal park start longing for a brand new day.

Daví poured two cups of coffee. His intensity made Merina think about the design of love and how she was yet to draw it. She added half-and-half to her full cup, stirring, sipping and finally leaning forward to ask, "Why the sage door?"

Circling his cup with both hands, Daví answered, "When I was looking at colors, it was the only one that didn't have an easy compliment. The color of your swimsuit feels very close."

Merina gazed into her cup and tried to conjure memories of sage and sunset. Reflections from the lanterns danced on the surface of her coffee, magnetized by their own shiny orbits. She re-stirred her lightened decaf, storming up a confusion of colors that she simply could not drink.

The moment Merina reached for her wallet, Elena appeared.

"It's on the house to repay for some *Saudades*."

"This was going to be my treat." Merina pulled out a twenty-dollar bill and asked, "Enough?"

Elena looked from Daví to Merina and with a smile replied, "Is it?"

The walk back to *Saudades* seemed half as long as the voyage to *Noirée*. Standing at the entrance to the courtyard, Merina thanked Daví for the swimsuit.

"You will think of me when you wear it and maybe…?"

"Maybe, what?"

"Maybe you will tell me how it fits."

"I can tell by looking at it. That's why I didn't need to try it on."

He turned his *azul* eyes toward the early morning sky.

"You got your wish, Daví."

Looking at her he asked, "Was there a shooting star?"

She studied the lines of his profile as if preparing for a test she wished to pass. "We spent the night together." She waved and quickly walked away.

The train jolted forward, tunneling through darkness into the bright light of a new and shining day. Driven to the dining car by hunger, Merina found a seat by the window. Looking outward, she saw an image of herself standing on firm ground, watching a locomotive make tracks cross country leaving her behind. While she was deciding whether to hitch a ride or board some coming train, a male voice could have broken through a dream. It asked, "Want to take this ride together?" She did not look at him, but her answer was black and white: "Only if you know exactly where we're going."

What If the Indians?

At around the middle of spring term during her sophomore year, Alura was tired of getting D's in high-school history. Lately, her concentration was helped by sitting close to the wall instead of near the window that looked onto Lexington Avenue in midtown Manhattan. The room was small and she could still see outside, but watching the static façades of four buildings was no where near as distracting as observing activities of people and transportation in the restless street below.

She thought carefully about everything Mr. Clarence said, despite the constant shock of his wild red hair and age spots that once passed for freckles on his hands. When she was honest with herself, she knew it was wrong to blame the three whitegirls who always sat in the front row and had a way of running the class. They talked fast and a lot. These traits could pass for intelligence unless you happened to read between the lines and found that they were blank.

Alura started wondering how it would feel to leave the back file of the room. Unspoken loyalty kept her sitting in that shadow with the two additional blackgirls in the class, which totaled twenty gifted females altogether.

What If the Indians?

In a meeting with Alura's mother on open-school night, Mr. Clarence said all Alura had to do was participate and apply herself because she could "do much better." The day they were covering Columbus, Amerigo Vespucci and also Martin Waldseemüller[2] was when Alura decided to try and elevate her grade. Unlike the three front-row girls, she raised her hand patiently and politely, waiting for Mr. Clarence to say, "Yes, Alura?"

Alura blurted out the beginning of her thoughts, "What if the Indians...?"

The whole class stared at her, mouths open, curious.

"What if the Indians had been able to resist Columbus?"

"What if, Alura? Tell us what you mean."

"You said that like I'm not part of *us*."

"Speak your mind."

Alura repeatedly tapped her pencil on the formica desk.

"What if everybody in the whole world just stayed home and there was no exploring or 'discovering?'" She made a pair of air quotes with her fingers.

The three front-row girls laughed loudly. Ralph Clarence fought to suppress a smile, winning by a slim margin. He pinched his lower lip and tilted his head to one side, the way he did when he was writing a homework assignment on the board. "But what about the isolation, Alura? Isolation can lead to massive ignorance."

"So can the opposite of isolation, but for some reason, we call that *civilization*."

---

[2] German cartographer who created the map, *Universalis Cosmographia*, in 1507, which names *America* after Amerigo Vespucci.

"Then what about freedom, Alura? Should anyone be able to live anywhere they want in the world? Are you sure you always want to live in America?"

"I'm talking about the beginning of this country, Mr. Clarence. I'm just trying to imagine how the whole world could have been better for everybody."

One of the three front-row girls, Shana, yawned loudly and said, "This is so fuckin' boring."

Alura raised her voice. "Because you didn't think of it, Shana?"

Shana whipped her head around. "Like you can prove that?"

"Like you can prove you *did*?" Jerusha, a back-row girl spoke up for the first time all term.

Mr. Clarence stood in the center of the room and slowly moved both flattened hands toward the floor. "Girls, calm down now." Wearily he said, "No cursing." He cut his eyes toward Shana, who cut her eyes right back at him.

"It's bullshit because the whole idea is impossible." Shana twisted uncomfortably toward Alura, who pushed toward the edge of her seat. "I mean, use your head *Alura*. If no one ever went anywhere, there wouldn't be any history..."

"And no history class." Jerusha made everyone laugh, even Mr. Clarence.

"Use *your* head, *Shana*." Alura mocked her classmate. "Of course there would be history. There might be more oral traditions and we wouldn't have a sense of world history, maybe, but it's not like everybody learns from the past anyway."

Mr. Clarence stared hard at Alura. "Sounds like you've just put me out of work, Alura. I had no idea you were so angry!"

Alura stood up and walked toward the door, stopping when she was face to face with her teacher.

"*Angry.*" She looked around and shrugged her shoulders. "I guess it's just that way sometimes, Mr. Clarence."

She smiled in his general direction, knowing without words that she would one day thank Ralph Clarence for teaching her to speak up and stand her ground. And then Alura left the room. She did not fail that class.

Sleep Away

There was blood. Its cause did not hurt as much as she had thought, that first time.

He was gentle—patient, making her lucky. Night protected him from seeing her blood and pain.

Who had told Glori she would bleed—anyone? Not her mother, Gina-Jeana. A teacher, then—the guidance counselor? Maybe Glori saw that fact in some book or magazine. She liked to read.

Glori was named after her grandmother, Gloria. Glori's first birth certificate added an *e* to the end of her name. Gina-Jeana attempted a correction. A *y* substitute was the result, like the dictionary word that stood for something strong. Somehow, the willful *i* prevailed.

As Glori grew, she did not inherit her grandmother's stature or wavy hair. Unlike her namesake, Glori was short, a bit heavy, and much darker skinned. Unable to cope with her own disappointment rationally, Gina-Jeana blamed those disparities on the birth certificate, unaware that her daughter faulted herself. Gina-Jeana's smooth complected, old-souled child had no self-sense of being pretty.

While locked beneath this manchild who pressed hard against her, Glori did not want to think of her grandmother or Gina-Jeana. It just did not seem right. He filled her up and called her name over and over like he might need help remembering her, perhaps hoping to be saved by all the repetition. Was she supposed to say his name back? Unsure, all she said was, "Yes?," again and again, praying for answers to her part in this exchange. Were there rules?

It was Glori's maiden summer at a camp in the Catskill Mountains. Children who lived far beyond peripheries of privilege came up for two-week stays from June through August. It was Glori's first time sleeping away from her home in the projects on the Lower East Side of Manhattan. After just three days, Glori became the arts and crafts specialist when her predecessor left suddenly after cursing out the assistant director. All that extra freedom and clean air — it was the first time Glori felt like glory.

Alden was a village leader at the boys' camp on the other side of the lake. His skin was dark like Glori's. Confidence edged the plainness of his clean-shaved face. He had a muscular physique like Glori's father, who she knew only from a photograph so well hidden there were times it would not let itself be found.

It was Alden who showed Glori how to build a fire when both camps took a three-mile, overnight hike begun late in the afternoon. He got the fire started. Glori kept it going. They sat across from each other in the circle formed around the blazes. The kids told jokes, ghost stories, and other harmless lies. Later than planned, the kids zipped themselves into sleeping bags that matched companion tee-shirts everyone wore each day — gray and yellow for the boys, orange and white for the girls. All were courtesy of the Urban Nature Fund.

Alden waited until the last voice grew quiet. Then, he made a place for himself at Glori's side and said, "You're sweet." Friends and relatives had told her that, but those words had a whole new meaning coming from this youthful man.

"You are so sweet." Alden moved closer so the sides of their thighs touched.

"Thank you." Glori forced herself to look directly at him.

"Can I kiss you?" He moved his lips within inches of hers.

"Just a little." She held perfectly still.

He laughed and kissed her fast. "Did you like it?"

What could she compare it to? Nothing, so Alden's question swirled around her like a summer squall. Finally, she shrugged and said, "It was okay."

Placing his hands on her shoulders, Alden said, "Here, let me make it better." He kissed her deeply. His fingertips were flames that licked her face, neck, and back. Soon, Glori pushed away from him.

"That's enough, Alden. I want to get some sleep."

"Glori—can I see you?"

"You know we're not supposed to. We're here to work."

He motioned toward the sleeping kids, boys on one side of the campsite, girls on the other.

"We are working. You don't like me?"

"I just met you. Good night." Glori got up and crawled into her sleeping bag beside Dayla, her village leader, who stared hard at Glori. Dark as it was, the severity in Dayla's light-brown eyes was clear. Her skin was the color of whole wheat, her face long and thin like the rest of her.

Glori started to say something, but Dayla pressed her index finger to her own lips then said, "I'll deal with you, tomorrow, Glori. Let these children sleep."

Sleep Away

Dayla turned over and away from Glori, tunneling into her sleeping bag like a boa constrictor.

Lying on her back, face to face with a sky full of silver stars, Glori wished to know the right thing to do, and for the strength to follow whatever that might be.

All the kids were even grouchier than usual the next morning, roused early from their first sleep completely at the mercy of outdoors. In this new wilderness, former critics of their cabins praised those friendly wooden structures as if they were villas. The children fought over boxed-cereal breakfasts and resisted cleaning up until Glori reminded them about their vulnerability to wild animals if they made a mess. She told them if they left a crumb behind, families of wolves, bears and mountain lions would stalk them all the way back to camp until they found only those kids who had been careless. Glori explained that because of endangered species laws, no one would be able to save those outlawed kids. That was how she was able to get them to pick up after themselves, come fully awake and put some energy into making it back to camp in time for lunch.

One mile down and two to go, the kids started singing camp songs they had learned — *The Ants Go Marching*; *The Itsy, Bitsy Spider*; and *100 Bottles of Beer on the Wall*, which was the finale that shifted focus from insects. Two miles down and one to go, they reached a steep hill that took them by surprise because they had coasted it in the other direction. Once the lake came into sight, the boys and girls had a second wind, which carried them to the forked path that separated their camps.

The girls raced ahead, creating sudden distance that gave Glori enough room to remember the night before, which was like a dream. She was used to dreaming about being kissed, imagining what kissing led to, and waking up before her imagination got confused in the details of secrets. Alden could clarify those mysteries if that was what she wanted.

"Glori."

She turned around and found herself facing Alden.

"Can we meet somewhere tonight? It'll be safer on your side. Just tell me where."

Place was easy. Glori's arts and crafts shop was next to the wide, open space of the dance lodge—she had a choice. But was she ready to know what Gina-Jeana knew about men, what everyone else her age and many younger seemed to know?

"It's too soon, Alden."

"Let's just talk, get to know each other."

"We can talk now. How old are you?"

"Twenty-three. You?"

"Eighteen. Aren't you kind of old to still be doing this?"

His voice rose slightly. "I have a real job the rest of the year. I do this out of the goodness of my heart." Alden placed a hand on his chest and said, "Listen, Glori. I should go. Like you said, we're here to work. What are we going to do?"

Gina-Jeana posed that question all the time. Glori turned it on herself: What should *I* do? In the midst of instinct, she listened as a familiar voice patted a place beside itself and said, "*Here, child. Come sit by me. It's alright to take some chances long as you can get out of anything you get into. You know right from wrong.*"

What would Gina-Jeana do without her after the summer, when she went away to college in upstate New York? What was the best thing to tell this man who wanted something from her that she had never given, but wanted to get rid of, simply to end all the wondering?

"Glori?" Alden's face was flooded with expectation.

Glori looked around, cautiously. "I'll meet you right here, soon as it gets dark."

Alden kissed her quickly, dashed off, and caught up with the boys.

Glori ran toward Dayla, who brought up the rear and started counting kids.

"Glori. There you are."

"Sorry, Dayla."

"Where were you?"

Glori shrugged. "Talking to someone."

"Alden."

"We were just...."

Dayla held up her hands. "I'm not your mother, Glori, but I do know where you're headed. I've been coming to this camp for five years now—I started as a camper. He's been here the last three. Alden comes up here for one reason."

"Okay, Dayla. I understand. If he's a problem, why do they keep letting him come back?"

"He only messes with the counselors. They're all over eighteen. No one's ever complained. Listen, we're almost back to camp. Get your act together, Glori. After lunch, we're taking the kids to the farm for dinner."

Glori was still full from breakfast, but she was not satisfied.

A black man and a white woman owned the farm. No kidding, their names were Adam and Eve. Love at first sight, they took this as a strong sign that they were created one for the other. This was due to the fact that they both made up their own religions. They had six kids, one from each continent except Antarctica, aged from four to seventeen. Big and blue, a converted barn was their house. It was the only building that broke up acre after acre of green fields filled with sweet white and yellow corn, oats, hay, and garden vegetables! The campers went crazy in the garden pulling up their first carrots, picking cucumbers and squash, Swiss chard, string beans, peas, lettuce, tomatoes. Strawberries. The children minded Eve when they reached the eggplants, cauliflower, and broccoli. She explained that they needed more time to grow up before anyone had a right to bother them.

One girl held up a carrot to Glori and asked, "Why's it so dirty?" The two of them wiped it off, found a spigot and washed it. By that time, the girl said, "Oh, I get it, now."

Adam, Eve, and their blended kids provided chicken, hot dogs, and burgers, while the campers grilled the fresh vegetables. All the kids played, fought, and sang until close to sundown when the food was ready. They sat down together at a picnic table in the calming presence and quelling heat of the sun. The campers eavesdropped on conversations between crickets, birds, and maple leaves disheveled by a gentle breeze. They heard a new language and learned that there was more than one solitary world. As the sun dipped beneath the horizon, Dayla rounded up the troops, flashlights in hands, and they began the forty-minute trip back to camp ably guided by a bluish half moon.

Glori tried to be so careful, slipping from the cabin with her red flashlight handy after dark.

"Glori!" Dayla called to her from across the circle at the center of their village.

Glori stood still, waiting for Dayla to approach her, which she did.

"Do I have to remind you about curfew?"

"You don't, but would you tell me something, Dayla?"

"What?"

"Have you always been a village leader?"

"No, why?"

"Were you ever a specialist?"

"Same as you, arts and crafts. So what?"

"Didn't you ever just need to go up to the shop in the evening to think about things, you know, just take a little time to yourself?"

"Walk with me just outside the circle, Glori. I don't want the kids to hear."

They went to a clearing where they could both keep their eyes on cabins and campers.

"No, I never took the time to think, but I have done exactly what you're about to do."

"*Exactly?*"

"Yes, with Alden."

"Oh. Are you two still...?"

"No, but you just be careful, girl. Make sure you protect yourself, not just from getting knocked up."

"Dayla, I have protection. What happened with you and him?"

"I felt so stupid when I found out he was screwing every other girl. I hate feeling stupid."

Glori looked toward the path that led away from their village, then back at Dayla, who shook her head and said, "I tried to tell you."

"I said I'd meet him, Dayla."

"You don't show up and he'll go right on to the next girl or back to the one before. I hope you don't end up feeling like I did."

"What should I do?"

"I should check on the kids, so that's what I'm going to do." Dayla returned to the inner circle.

Absentmindedly, Glori walked toward the meeting place. The sky was clear and the half moon bright enough that she left her flashlight off. After a month at camp, her footsteps fit along this path. Critter-chatter was a familiar substitute for cars whizzing along the East River Drive a world away, down on the Lower East Side.

"Glori!" Alden whispered and stood before her on the path. "You're late."

"You're wearing a watch?"

He laughed nervously. "You're right. I'm not. I just know what time I left camp. Seemed like it took forever for you to get here."

"I was talking with Dayla."

"What did she have to say?"

"Guess."

"So, she told you."

"About what?"

"Listen, Glori — where are we going?"

She changed direction, leading away from the village, toward her shop. Alden followed close behind her on the narrow path. Gauzy clouds hid the moon's half face and Glori switched on her flashlight.

"You afraid of the dark?" Alden put his arm around Glori and she stopped to answer him, eye to eye.

"I'm not afraid of anything."

They walked quietly, but to Glori, there no such thing as silence. She had a certain peace with her own thoughts, a constant awareness of her soul, and she stayed attentive to the chattering of critters pacing through the night. While listening for their guidance, she played ping pong with her choices. Feeling neither doom nor excitement, she struggled to name what she did feel. She was certain that name would have met her on its own terms had Alden been able to endure the absence of words, words, words.

"So, are you going to tell me what you and Dayla were talking about?" He squeezed beside Glori on their tightening path.

"Things we have in common."

"You both seem very different to me."

"There is one thing in common between all of us on this side of the lake, Alden."

Alden stopped, suddenly. "I like females, Glori. I *love* them."

"And I know I like men."

"*How* do you know?"

"I think about them all the time."

They held hands. Walked wordlessly until they came to a large sign that read, "Glori's Arts & Crafts Shop," in bright pink letters. Finger-painted, overlapping hands—blue, orange, yellow, and green—pointed to the words. The shop, itself, was a small building camouflaged by brown and green paint that meshed with the woods.

"That's your spot?"

Glori nodded.

"You're alright, Glori. Aren't we going in?" Alden took a giant step to the threshold.

"No. Over there." She jutted her chin toward a large, open structure roughly thirty yards away.

They climbed seven steps that led to the dance studio. Arms curled around each other, they walked to the farthest corner where, independently, they peeled off their clothes. That fabric fell to the slatted floor and made

their bed—a place for them to sleep away, bathed in light left over from a
blue and waning half moon.

Flip Turn

Windows made of beveled glass wrapped around the Mexican restaurant, which enjoyed prominence on the waterfront. Its neighbors were an estuary and in the distance, a palisade. Despite this desirable location, a long line of enterprises had failed to survive the critical first year in business along that short stretch of property. It was as if an elemental spirit refused to be owned or occupied for any length of time. To date, the restaurant had endured for thirteen months, but it could not shake the vibe that always lingered in the air. Some days, that same force formed a filmy barrier layer on the surface of the water. That effect could be seen only by those with the keenest powers of perception who happened to be looking when timely wakes spewed forth their warnings.

A clouding sky was resident the evening in late January when Blessine and Brick walked upstairs to the bar so they could avoid waiting for a table. Blessine had the longer legs and she took the stairs two at a time, straightening her pair of short, black braids once she reached the top. Brick adjusted his rectangular eyeglasses when he caught up with his wife and took her by the hand. She had the darker skin, which always warmed to his touch.

They had wanted to try this place sooner, but other plans had always intervened. It was a Friday night and weary from a week of draining work, Blessine and Brick left work early and arrived at happy hour. Neither of them drank, but they were glad to escape the heavy dinner crowd, which was expected by the forty-first hour of each work week.

They approached a green upholstered window seat in the southeast corner of the bar. Blessine braked before an empty table to peer outside.

"Brick, are those houseboats?"

Brick sat down and patted the cushion beside him, soon joined by his wife.

"Yeah. One of the guys I work with from time to time called them *floating homes.*"

A young *chicana* server introduced herself as Margo and told them about the day's special: grilled lime-cilantro sea bass with a four-bean salad and saffron rice.

Brick said, "That sounds good," and ignored his menu. Blessine opened hers and Margo vowed to come back soon.

The bobbing motion of the houseboats hypnotized Blessine. To steady herself, she pressed against the back of her seat, but the hard, cold, plastic cushion cut right across her shoulder blades. Sunlight flickered between sluggish clouds further compromising her sense of balance. Leaning against her husband's side and sitting slightly forward were welcome anchors.

Blessine opened the window and noticed someone walking down the gangway about thirty yards from where they sat. The dock cried out with each footfall in companionship with pain.

"I wonder what it's like to live there, Brick. We both love water."

"True, Bless, but all I can see is W-O-R-K. Look at that dock." He craned closer to the window. "See those pieces of plywood that are coming up? It's not safe."

"Say most of them are fixer-uppers, Brick, would you say they're more or less expensive than buying a regular house?"

"It's a whole different environment, Bless. There's no comparison. The sales price might be a lot lower, but I'm sure there's a lot of maintenance and other hidden 'oh-by-the-ways' that would come up once you'd already gotten into it."

Blessine put her arm around her husband's shoulders and murmured, "It looks so peaceful, Brick, like every day would feel like a vacation."

"Baby, I'll take you where you want to go. You know the reputation this town has for being conservative. Remember, that's at least part of the reason it's taken us this long to eat here." He looked around, trying to sense whether they did or did not fit in. So far, the coast felt clear. "I don't know how 'peaceful' it would be for people who look like us. I mean really, Bless, have you ever heard of any black people living on a *houseboat*?"

"I never thought about it, Brick. We are getting ready to move, right? Being 'firsts' is almost getting old for us. Why did we come here *this* evening?"

"Same reason we go to any restaurant, Bless — to eat the food."

Margo returned with two glasses of water. "Need more time?"

Resting her hands on top of the menu, Blessine introduced herself and Brick then asked, "Do you know anything about those houseboats, Margo?" She nodded toward the windows. The sun was locked behind a heavy bank of clouds.

Poised to take their order, Margo looked outside. "They don't come up that often, but one's for sale. It's over on the other side of the marina. You might be able to see the sign."

Brick leaned back and crossed an ankle to his knee. "My wife is very good at seeing signs."

Blessine playfully poked her husband of ten years in the ribs and asked Margo, "Have you ever thought of living in one?"

"Never."

"May I ask why?"

"I get seasick."

"Is that it?"

"Well, you know, you only own the houseboat. You have to rent a berth from the owner of the marina."

"See, Bless. Dealing with a landlord is only the tip of that iceberg."

Blessine murmured, "With global warming, they say ice caps are melting...."

"But Baby, look how long that took!"

Margo whispered, "They say there's a spell over this whole area." She dropped her order pad and deftly caught it mid air. A bit louder she said, "Take your time."

"I'm ready, Margo. I'll have the tortilla soup-chile relleno-chicken tamale combo with black beans instead of pintos, please."

"That's the only thing I've never tried." Margo scooped up the menus and headed toward the kitchen.

Brick drank half a glass of water and asked his wife, "How was your swim this morning?"

"Still working on those flip turns."

"I'll always admire you for learning how to swim at thirty-five, Bless. I can't believe it's been a year already. I'd like to do something big like that for my fortieth this year."

"You'll come up with something." She squeezed his hand gently and glanced outside. Out on bail, the sun had sunk beneath one heavy cloud and slimly held its place above an expanse of hungry fog. "Looking out at the estuary, I was thinking about how flip turns don't make sense in open water. Maybe you're right about houseboats, Brick. Maybe it just wouldn't make sense."

"Two things, Bless." He held up one finger. "First, you know that photo of yours I love so much—the one on the wall in my office of the llama in that field of sheep?"

Blessine nodded, smiling sadly. "I still feel sorry for the llama even though it looked so stuck up. It must have felt out of place."

"Exactly. Something tells me that's how we'd feel in that houseboat 'community.'"

"What's the second thing?"

"Bless, I do construction work all day. When we do buy a house, I want it to be finished. I can *smell* how much effort it would take to keep one of those places together. Dry rot's got to be a major problem—and leaks.

"Speaking of *spells*, those conditions alone spell major rebuilding, so there's an answer to your question about price. It would be a major false economy of scale.

"Then there's access, walking along those rickety docks. Let's not even think about inspections and building permits or code."

"Aren't you getting way ahead of things, Brick? We've never even been on a floating home! Can't we just have a look?"

"You don't believe anything I've said, do you, Bless?"

♪ 67 ♪

"I do, I trust your judgment, Brick, but you know me. I'm visual. I teach art at the college, remember? Some things I just have to see." Her eyes sparkled with excitement while her lips remained in one straight line. Then the sides of her mouth curled up, dulling the glitter in her eyes, freezing time in one dynamic moment.

The food came. Brick started with his sea bass before moving to the four-bean salad and tasting the saffron rice. He could never be caught mixing discrete foods. Blessine finished her small cup of soup before cutting her chile relleno into small pieces, doing the same with the chicken tamale, and skewering the combined morsels onto the end of her fork.

It grew dark outside and lights came on in waves across the water. A half moon carved its path through clouds and fog above the distant hills. Blessine and Brick ate in the center of their silence.

Distorted reflections on the rippling water captured Blessine's attention. A memory of snorkeling in Kauai and swimming with colored schools of fish illuminated her imagination.

Steam squeezed into the air, proving that the wintery water in the swimming pool was warm. Alleluia! The elusive band of blue directly above the water's surface, immediately beneath the visible air, was a hue that soothed the swimmer's animated soul. In the comfort of the steam, the swimmer stroked through the water as the sun rose, splitting light across the quicksilver surface. Feeling each kick, each breath, each movement of arm and hand, each twisting of the neck, the swimmer prepared to meet the wall. She knew what to do, had rehearsed it in her mind, had looked at pictures and memorized series of instructions. She knew what to do, how to do it – even when – but could she become the flip turn?

What small thing will make all the difference in the world, Blessine?

And when it rained, droplets danced along the supple surface of your skin...

"Blessine!" Brick placed his hand firmly on her shoulder. "Margo's asking if we want dessert." He looked around and raised his voice. "Way too many people in here now."

"It's raining, Brick." Blessine nodded toward the window and murmured, "Let's get the check."

Margo collected their empty plates and walked toward the cash register.

Three medics took the table beside Blessine and Brick—a thin white woman with dark hair, a muscular man who looked Asian and Latino, and a black man whose head was shaved. The woman was the talker.

"You both owe me five dollars—pay up." She extended her hand. "Don't act like you don't understand English all of a sudden."

The black man said, "I suppose you want exact change."

"You got it, Harper?"

"Yeah." He dug deep into his left pocket while the other man slammed five singles on the table.

"Damn, Lucía, don't you feel sorry for that guy?" The Asian-Latino man folded his arms across his chest and nodded toward the marina. "He lived alone. Nobody seemed to know anything about him. He didn't even have a dog."

"Carl, I feel for people who get help when they need it and use whatever good sense they've got."

"How do you know he didn't do both those things?" Harper folded his hands on the table.

"I don't, Harper. All I know is what you know. We've gotten called next door damn near every Friday night to pull that drunk so-and-so out of the estuary. I told you one day he'd drown, and finally, I'm right. But you know what seems strange to me?"

"You're gonna tell us." Carl started tapping his right foot.

"Now, you'd think there would be a lot of swimmers over there." She tilted her head in the direction of the houseboats. "So, you'd think someone would have been able to save him."

Harper said, "We don't know why he drowned, Luci. He could have had some other problem."

"Or maybe he was an asshole." Lucía bent her right arm over the back of the chair. "I'm just saying."

Carl asked, "How long's his place been for sale?"

Lucía squinted. "First time I noticed the sign."

"Nah." Harper waved a hand. "It's been up as long as I can remember."

"Hey." Carl beckoned to his partners. The three of them leaned in toward the center of their table. Blessine and Brick tilted in the direction of their neighbors. "I just heard this place is going out of business within the month. I don't think the workers know it yet."

Angling back in her chair, Lucía said, "That doesn't surprise me. There's something about this whole little area here that is crying out to be 'un-disturbed.'"

"Too late for that now, isn't it?" Carl signaled a male server, who came over and took their orders for drinks.

The new guy stopped at Blessine and Brick's table. He asked, "How was everything?"

Brick rubbed his middle and said, "Hit the spot."

Blessine looked across the estuary, staking out their neighborhood on the other side. Convinced that she had mapped it out precisely, she replied. "We really love the view."

Music for the Dream

Slate-blue sky roughs up with clouds that protect Naniki[3] while she rows across the sea. Supine, her body is the boat, her arms and legs the oars, but she has no awareness of bones or skin, and water is her blood. Watching the soft motion of the graying clouds, she surrenders her own movement to the tides and gentle wind that play upon the flutey air. The sound of gentle waves cautions her against sleep until she returns to solid land that stands for what is safe.

Eyes closed, Naniki dreams the same life she lives in full sight. Like birds ascending slowly, her lids open to behold a hole up in the heavens. Startled, her reflex is to find her feet, but the water is too deep. So, Naniki treads water frantically while studying the hole. It widens, taking on the size and shape of the island, Choreto, where she has always lived — the only place that exists for her. Its form is as intimate as her heartbeat, which she feels most strongly while in her home at the highest point of the island. From there, she watches over animals and fish. From there, she blesses fresh, clean water to drink and flora for nutrition.

---

[3] "Spirit," or "to be active," in the Taíno language.

Feeling stranded, Naniki must regain her rhythm with the water. Formidable powers of the ocean dawn on her, requiring her to move and breathe a certain way to protect herself from drowning and disappearing into a hole that is the sea.

She feels clumsy, making her way back to the sand, awkwardly shoving water out of her way with her arms, kicking it behind her as salt stings her eyes and both ears clog up. Listening intently and seeing insightfully become her guides through the water, through the currents of her life.

Trying to stand, Naniki gulps water, breathing out when she should take air in. Wiping water from her eyes, she turns round and round, looking for the familiar place on sand where it is her custom to watch the sea from the land's point of view. She cannot sight that place. Is it gone? Is this salty water on her face a set of tears?

Looking up, lightning strikes within her bloodstream as she notices that the hole is exactly the same as before. This cannot be. Clouds are always moving, changing, clearing away all things that do not belong, except this new aperture that stays fixed in the sky slapping the face of the traveling sun.

Naniki starts to sink. Head under water, it is calm enough for her to think. Blurred vision is a shield that allows her to make way toward the land. She feels without seeing, driven by the heart-mind of Choreto with force as strong as birth.

Dumped onto the shore, Naniki wipes her eyes with two balled fists, copper against the pewter sand. Yellow cloth covers the female parts of her rounded body. Trailing toward her shoulders, crinkled, black hair stirs in a breeze that whispers questions about the island staying hidden.

Facing the hole, there is no question that it is watching her, alone, where she sits on the shore. Slowly standing to steady the trembling in her legs, Naniki straightens up and takes a few steps away from the shore. She faces the hills and runs toward home, tripping on stones, leaves, and fallen berries. Naniki has no words for how it feels to stumble along paths that have always touched her feet as if their dirt were skin. Along the way, she crosses paths with the brothers, Jibaro and Caguama, and the elders, Liani and Ita. As usual, they all smile. Stopping, she waits for them to say something about the hole until she realizes that none of them are looking up. It occurs to her that she has never seen anyone else floating supine on the surface of the sea. They all offer the customary Choreto greeting, *Bi guarico,*[4] "We are glad you were born." Unperturbed, the group moves past Naniki, gliding as smoothly across the land and through the air as she used to travel through water.

She asks herself, *"Should I tell them?,"* surprised by the swiftness of the answer, *"What would be the purpose?"* Another question tumbles through Naniki's mind providing enough momentum to see her home with no memory of how she got there. Four words pound on her brain as if it is a sacred drum. They translate to, *"What should I do?"*

Naniki's dwelling is beside *yabisi*, the tree that lives forever. She imagines its twisted roots reaching down to minerals and crystals that look up to land as land looks up to sky, all that gazing—why? The pale yellow dwelling is one, large simple room of four walls with a single window that keeps watch on the sea.

Sitting beside her home, Naniki looks toward the endless water, reflecting on what might lie on the other side of the hole that breathes new

---

[4] Literally, *life/beginning/first; come/come here.*

wind, encircling her. Her skin begins to itch. Instead of scratching it, she stands and runs at a slow, even pace away from one questionable force toward another that is familiar. The orange sun slides toward the blue horizon and takes tiny breaths of planet-filled air. Approaching the end of the island, a new beginning of the sea, Naniki hears the patterns of a song she recognizes as music for the dream. Perfectly still, Naniki interprets a message from Choreto:

I bring this new language to you from my travels. You notice everything, Naniki, and you are one with motion. That opening you see in the sky is for you. I can take you through it and show you what lies Outside, beyond this Choreto, but you must know one thing: If you come with me, Choreto might be 'discovered.' I will explain so you can understand.

All we know is good. Outside, there is not-good.

All we know is happy. Outside, there is not-happy.

All we know is love. Outside, there is not-love.

We live and re-live. Outside, they die.

Outside, there is an evil thing called 'war.'

We know that we have everything we need. If we are 'discovered,' others will come here and everything will change.

You must decide right now, Naniki, whether you will stay or come with me. Always, I keep going. Your opening grows smaller.

This is the first time Choreto has spoken to Naniki like this. Naniki knows she is meant to listen without adding her own words or thoughts. She has always had a sense of being *chosen* and knows that this also means that she is free to choose.

Naniki does not like the sounds of the words, *discover*, *die*, and *war*. Dipping her fingers into the surf, she tries to wash these unwelcome letters from the insides of her ears and their meanings start to fade.

Looking to the glowing, golden sky she sees that the hole has molded itself to the shape of her own body. The likeness of that distant form makes her feel confined. Reflecting on Choreto's words makes deficient sense of them.

Diving into the sea, Naniki regains her rhythm and swims away from all unwanted winds of change.

Acknowledgments

It's taken a long time to admit that writing is indeed a solitary enterprise. Characters and imagination are satisfying allies, but the actual work of translating ideas comes down to discipline. I find process and completion equally gratifying with the reward of delivering a finished book to readers. It is a tremendous pleasure to discover the creativity and insights that an audience brings to the interactive experience of reading books.

Robert N. Zagone, thank you for reading *Music for the Dream* as a manuscript, and for continuing to treat my writing seriously. Mary K., thank you for being an early reader and for introducing me to Dorothy. Dorothy, thank you for inviting me to visit your book club, and Ethel, thank you for having that visit catered! June, thank you for hosting a meeting with your group. Babs, thank you for reading between the lines so accurately and for featuring *Tanner Blue* as a selection for your club.

Betsy Chen, thank you for introducing me to Ruth Wittman who generously made time to read *Tanner Blue* and *Music*. Betsy, thank you for making me feel welcome and understood when I visited your book club.

Lisa Diane, thank you for the interview on The Rapturous Reader/blogtalkradio to celebrate Black History Month this year. The time flew by because of your professionalism, thoughtful questions, and engaging personality.

My friends know who they are and I treasure their confidence.

Mom, Kenny, and Fred — thank you for continuing to believe in me and for wishing me good luck all the time. Like the factual solitude of writing, good luck is a natural companion of success.

www.ingramcontent.com/pod-product-compliance
Lightning Source LLC
Chambersburg PA
CBHW030150200626
46812CB00016B/1782